Up for the Challenge

WRITTEN BY LEIGH OLSEN

DISNEP PRESS

New York

Content of book was developed in consultation with Lilly USA, LLC
and is funded by Lilly USA, LLC.

First Edition
10 9 8 7 6 5 4 3 2

ISBN 978-1-4231-2480-1
V475-2873-0-13235

PRINTED IN USA
LD85651 07/2013 LILLY IS A REGISTERED TRADEMARK OF ELI LILLY AND COMPANY.
ALL RIGHTS RESERVED.

**Looking for tips on family life with type 1 diabetes?
Visit www.spooonful.com/type1**

For more Disney Press fun, visit www.disneybooks.com

SUSTAINABLE
FORESTRY
INITIATIVE

Certified Chain of Custody
Promoting Sustainable Forestry

www.sfiprogram.org
SFI-01054
The SFI label applies to the text stock

Up for the Challenge

Chapter 1

Allie Campbell could hardly contain herself. "You've got this!" she shouted enthusiastically from the sideline. Allie clenched her fists at her sides, bouncing slightly on her toes as she anxiously watched her teammate, Jo, dribble the soccer ball down the field.

It was the third soccer game of the season for the Tornados, and they were playing at home. The score was tied with only a minute left in the game. Allie's best friend, Jo

Mendes, was the Tornados' best player. If anyone could pull off a last-minute goal, it was Jo.

Allie watched as her friend sped past the other team's defenses, her long brown ponytail flying. Jo wound up for a kick and sent the ball sailing into the upper left corner of the net. *Score!* The referee blew his whistle to signify the end of the game.

Allie shrieked, pumping her fist into the air. "We won!" she exclaimed. Allie grabbed her fellow sidelined teammates and raced onto the field. The girls encircled Jo and the rest of the team in a massive hug.

Allie usually felt like she fit right in with her teammates, but today was different. They were all dressed in their Kelly green uniforms, while Allie wore her favorite pair of worn-out skinny jeans, sheepskin boots, and her coziest hoodie to keep her warm against the early September chill.

Allie wasn't dressed in her uniform because she hadn't played in today's game. She had just been diagnosed with type 1 diabetes a few days earlier and she didn't feel ready to get back on the field yet. Not that her teammates knew the real reason she'd sat out the game. She'd told them she was sick, and they'd believed her. After all, she'd been missing school and practice for the past few days. Plus, technically, she was telling the truth. She *was* sick. She would tell them the truth about her diabetes when she was ready. Right now, she was having a hard enough time processing her diagnosis herself. She definitely wasn't up for telling other people about it.

But even with all the thoughts and worries about diabetes running through her head, Allie couldn't stay away from this weekend's game. She loved soccer and her teammates too much to miss a big match like this so early in the season.

When the group hug disbanded, Jo leaped over to Allie and flung her arm around her best friend's shoulders. "How ya feelin', Al?" Jo asked, using her favorite nickname for Allie.

"Oh, fine," Allie said, brushing off the subject with a smile. "Nice job out there!"

"Thanks," Jo answered.

Allie, like the rest of her teammates, was in eighth grade. She had moved to Chestnut Ridge late last year from a nearby town, where she had been one of the stars of her soccer team—a starting center midfielder. The Tornados were Chestnut Ridge's all-girl travel soccer team. They played teams all over the state, and they had a reputation for being pretty good. Allie had heard of the Tornados in her old town and was excited to play for them, but she had moved to Chestnut Ridge too late in the year to try out for the team.

Luckily, Allie and Jo had bonded during

their ridiculously boring seventh-grade history class. They had been inseparable ever since, and had spent the whole summer kicking around the ball together. Jo quickly realized what a great soccer player her new best friend was. Before the start of the school year, Jo convinced Coach Rebecca to let Allie have a shot at the team. After a stellar tryout, Coach Rebecca was happy to make an exception and add Allie to the roster. But since this season's starters had already been chosen, Allie had to be on the second string. Not that she minded. Truthfully, she was just happy to be part of the team.

Allie and Jo were kind of an unusual pair. Allie was a bit of a wallflower — sweet-natured and thoughtful, but with a whole lot of spirit beneath her shy exterior. Jo, on the other hand, was outgoing, full of energy and spunk. Through her friendship with Jo, Allie found herself coming out of her shell.

Allie and Jo joined the rest of their team gathered around their coach. Coach Rebecca was young—a recent college graduate who had played soccer for her university. She had shoulder-length, light brown curls and a perma-smile on her face. She was the ideal coach—super supportive and energetic, while at the same time, just one of the girls. She had been where they were, and she always seemed to understand the girls' troubles, on or off the field.

"Great job today, guys!" Coach Rebecca exclaimed. "The Tornados have three wins under our belts so far this season! We're undefeated! If we keep this up, we'll be on our way to the league championships, and I think that's cause for celebration. So, who's up for some ice cream?"

The team burst into cheers. Except for Allie. She hesitated for just a moment, thinking about the eating plan she had to follow.

She was working with her diabetes team to learn how to work in things like ice cream, but she didn't know enough yet to do it on her own. For now, she was watching what she ate and her dietitian was helping her and her mom plan her meals and snacks. And the way she ate was just the beginning of the adjustments Allie had to make. It felt like everything had changed the day she was diagnosed with diabetes.

Allie thought back to that trip to the doctor's office. Her pediatrician had sent her to see the pediatric endocrinologist, Dr. Cass. Dr. Cass was a stylish young doctor with a friendly smile. She pulled up a chair in front of Allie and looked her in the eye.

"Your test results show that you have an illness called type 1 diabetes, Allie," Dr. Cass had said. "Your blood glucose is much higher than it should be."

Allie remembered feeling like the wind had been knocked out of her. She hadn't known what to say, much less what to think. Allie hadn't known anything about diabetes, and she certainly didn't know what blood glucose was.

Everything after that had felt like a whirlwind. A diabetes nurse had come in and taught Allie about insulin and how it affects blood glucose levels. She had learned how to use a glucose meter to test her blood sugar and how to give herself an insulin shot. She'd had to learn about the symptoms of high and low blood sugar. Her nurse had even given her a logbook to write down her glucose levels and the food she ate, to share with her medical team. Then she'd been signed up for diabetes education classes, where she'd learn all kinds of important stuff like monitoring her levels, how to adjust her insulin dosage, how foods affect blood sugar, and a whole lot more. Allie had felt totally overwhelmed. Luckily, her parents were there, and she knew she could call her diabetes team any time she needed their help. But it was a lot of information to process, and at this stage in the game, Allie felt like a complete newbie. Something like eating ice cream with friends suddenly seemed a lot more complicated than it would have a week ago.

"Allie! Hey, Allie! You coming or what?"

Allie looked up, her thoughts snapping back to the soccer field. Jo was standing by her parents' car, waving at her.

"Uh, why don't you go on ahead without me?" Allie called. "I'll hitch a ride with my parents!"

Jo shrugged and hopped in her parents' car. The parking lot was already emptying out.

Allie couldn't decide whether or not to go for ice cream with the team. She wanted to be with her friends, to celebrate their win. But she didn't want them asking any questions. Maybe she'd just say her stomach hurt.

Just then, Allie felt an arm around her shoulder. It was her mother, who had finally made her way down the bleachers with Allie's dad.

"Hey, sweetie," Mrs. Campbell said. Allie's mom wore a red zip-up fleece and jeans. The two looked alike—long, wavy blond hair, huge brown eyes, and freckled button noses.

Allie's dad was a tall, dark-haired, bearded bear of a guy, who was dressed in a hooded sweatshirt, his university name splashed across the front.

"So, do you want to head over to the ice-cream parlor or go on home?" Allie's dad asked with an understanding look on his face. "We're up for whatever you are."

Allie sighed, then put on a brave face. "I'd like to go," she said. "But I think I'll skip the ice cream." She willed a smile onto her face to show her parents she meant it.

"All right, then, Alligator," said Mr. Campbell. "Let's go."

Chapter 2

At the ice-cream parlor, Allie found her teammates gathered around the outdoor picnic tables, cones and cups of ice cream in hand. Allie's parents walked off to the side, joining the other adults in conversation.

Allie got a bottled water from the concession window and plopped down next to Jo, who sat by Helen Simons, the team sweeper. Across the table, Julie Chang and Marnie

Anderson, the Tornados' star goalie, perched on a wooden bench. Allie considered herself friends with everyone on the team, but she found that she spent most of her off-the-field time with these four.

"Hey, Allie!" greeted Julie. "No ice cream?"

"Nah," Allie said, "I'm not feeling up to it today."

"Makes sense. When I'm sick, *nothing* sounds good to me," said Marnie.

"Yeah, that must be it," Allie said. She felt a twinge of regret about her little white lie.

"I was just in the middle of telling these girls an *amazing* story," Marnie continued. "You've *got* to hear this." In addition to being a great goalie, Marnie was an avid drama club girl. She had a huge personality, and she was always making people laugh. Her hand gestures were animated, and her short, brunette ponytail bobbed as she told her latest story. The girls laughed as they listened along.

Allie adored her new friends here. There was really nothing like being part of a team.

"Hey, are you guys going to Charlene's party next weekend after the game?" Jo asked. "I can't wait! She goes all out for her sleepovers."

Charlene Jackson was a veteran member of the Tornados, and her birthday was just around the corner. The whole team was invited to her house to celebrate.

"You bet I'll be there!" said Helen. "You know I'm always up for a party, especially if there's pizza involved." Helen was tiny—not quite five feet tall, with a blond pixie haircut. You would never suspect that a girl like her could scarf an entire pizza in one sitting.

"I'm coming!" said Marnie. "I can't wait!"

Once again, Allie hesitated. She didn't know if she'd be able to sleep over somewhere so soon after her diagnosis. She nodded, smiling vaguely, to indicate that she'd be there—just to avoid any questions. She would have to talk to her parents about it.

"I can't make it," said Julie, staring down into her ice cream.

"Aw, boo!" Marnie cried. "Why not?"

"I . . . I have something to tell you guys," Julie started. "My mom got a new job across the state, in Fairfield, and we're moving."

"What!?" Helen exclaimed.

"We just found out a couple of weeks ago," Julie added, tucking a piece of her short, dark hair behind her ear. "I've been putting off telling you guys. It stinks."

"Oh my gosh, no!" said Allie.

"Oh, Julie!" Marnie hugged her friend. "Can't you stay here and at least finish out the season with us? You can stay with me!"

Julie smiled sadly. "I wish," she said. "But I think I'd miss my family too much. Believe me, I am going to miss you guys like *crazy*."

"Will you come visit us?" Jo asked.

"Of course!" Julie said. "It's a few hours' drive, but I will totally come back whenever I can."

Allie was in shock. "What are we going to do without you?" she asked.

"It's funny that you ask, actually," Julie said, a small smile starting to form on her face. "I was talking to Coach Rebecca about that. I mean, of course I'm super upset about leaving. Don't even get me started on going to a new school! But I *am* really excited about who'll be replacing me as center midfielder. . . ."

"Who?!" asked Jo.

Julie smiled. "Allie!"

Marnie let out a squeal of excitement.

Allie wasn't sure she'd heard right. "Me?" she asked. "But I'm not supposed to be a starter! I just joined you guys!"

"Yeah, you," Julie said. "You're an awesome player! You totally deserve it."

"What about Aisha?" Allie asked. She was sure Aisha Panchal would get the spot. She was already a starter for the Tornados, playing right midfielder. But she had made it known she would rather play center, and she'd been on the Tornados for years. Allie was sure Aisha would be given preference for the position. Plus, Allie didn't know how she would react to Allie playing her coveted position. Aisha could have kind of an . . . attitude, sometimes. Allie had tried to stay off her radar, but she supposed now it wouldn't be quite so easy. Allie hoped Aisha wouldn't mind that she was playing center mid.

"Aisha's great at right mid, right where she is," Julie said frankly. "Plus, you've done an awesome job every time you've subbed in for me. Your speed on the field is ridiculous. And I'm sure Coach hates to see such talent getting wasted on the sidelines! She told me herself she thinks your ballhandling skills are some of the best on the team."

"I don't know what to say," Allie replied, flattered by the compliments but upset about her friend's departure. At the same time, she felt her nerves zap to life. What about her diabetes? What would it be like playing as a starter? Would she be able to get back on the field soon enough?

Not wanting her friends to see her concern, Allie wiped her worries from her face. She smiled at her friend. "I don't want you to leave!" she said genuinely. "We won't be the same without you."

"I know, but you should be excited!" Julie said, reassuringly placing her hand on Allie's arm. "It's so awesome for you! And don't worry about me. My new town has a great travel team. They've won the league championship the last two years. And they've only lost one game this season. And they happen to be in need of a midfielder. I'll even get to play you guys!"

"Won't that be crazy?" asked Helen, a look of excitement on her face. "Coach Rebecca thinks we might be good enough this year to make the league championship. Maybe your new team will make it again, too!"

The Tornados' league consisted of seven teams around the state. At the end of the season, the two teams with the most wins played each other in a final game to determine who was the best in the league. If Julie's new team was as good as she said, Allie might be facing off against her friend for the trophy!

Allie's head was swimming. Everything seemed to be changing all at once. She was sad to see her friend leave. At the same time, the prospect of playing as a starter both thrilled and terrified her. She knew she was a good soccer player. But this diabetes thing had completely thrown her for a loop. She didn't know the first thing about playing with diabetes yet. Could she possibly have any *more* on her mind?

A few days ago, the prospect of being a starter would have been nothing but fabulous news. But now, was she up to the challenge?

Chapter 3

Allie and her parents got home late that afternoon, just as dusk was settling in. The three of them sat together in the living room, the TV humming and glowing in the background.

"You had a big day today, huh, kiddo?" asked Mr. Campbell.

"Yeah," Allie said. "I was bummed not to be on the field, but I'm just not sure I'm ready for it yet."

"You'll be back out there soon enough, hon," said Mrs. Campbell.

"Did you at least have fun seeing your friends?" Mr. Campbell asked.

"Oh, yeah," Allie said. "But Julie just told us she's moving. I guess I'm going to play starting center mid now." She said this flatly, still not sure how she felt about it.

"Oh, sweetie! It's so sad that Julie's leaving," said Mrs. Campbell.

"Yeah, that's a shame," said Mr. Campbell. "And you know how much we like Julie, but starting center mid? That's what you played back in Schaumfield."

"Yes, that piece of it does seem like a silver lining!" Mrs. Campbell agreed.

"I don't know," Allie said, shrugging. "I'm not sure I'll be up for it."

"What do you mean?" Mrs. Campbell asked. "You're such a great soccer player."

Allie felt tears rising in her eyes. Her

throat tightened as she tried to keep from crying.

"Oh, sweetie," Mrs. Campbell said, scooting next to Allie on the couch and throwing her arm around her. "You're going to be able to play just fine. We're learning to manage your diabetes one day at a time. You just need your confidence back."

"And we have total confidence in you already," said Mr. Campbell. "There's nothing you can't face if you put your mind to it."

Allie couldn't help but let loose a tear. She quickly wiped it off her cheek using the back of her hand. She had never felt less confident in herself. The worst part was that, although she knew she would eventually be able to manage her diabetes on her own, she had no choice but to learn to live with it. She couldn't just get rid of it and move on. She was angry that she had no control over the situation. If it weren't for her diabetes, she'd be thrilled about playing center mid. But now . . . she just felt lost.

"It's going to be okay, Alligator," Mr. Campbell said. "Your mom and I are going to that diabetes education class with you tomorrow, and we'll learn even more how you can still be your best out on the field."

Allie had already been to two diabetes education classes, where her nurse educator had taught her about monitoring her blood sugar—like when to check her level and what the numbers on the blood glucose meter meant. She had also learned about insulin and how it works, as well as how to determine dosages, things like that. Tomorrow's class would focus on healthy eating and physical activity.

"I know," Allie sighed. "I'm sure it'll be fine. I guess it'll just take some getting used to."

"Chin up, sweet pea," Mrs. Campbell said, rubbing her daughter's back. "You're going to play starter! Things are looking up for you."

Allie wished she felt the same way.

The next morning, Allie climbed into the car with her mom and dad. Her dad offered to sit in the backseat so Allie could have shotgun and control over the radio, but Allie wasn't much in the mood for music.

Fifteen minutes later, the car pulled up to the children's hospital, where Allie's diabetes education class would take place. They parked in the cavernous parking garage and made their way to a small conference room that had been set up with a few tables and chairs for the families in attendance. Allie and her parents were the first ones there.

A friendly looking woman stood writing something on a giant white dry-erase board. When the woman spotted the Campbells, she immediately approached them.

"Hi! I'm your dietitian for the day. My

name's Melanie." Allie had had a nurse educator for her previous two classes and didn't recognize Melanie. She was middle-aged with a kind smile. Her dirty-blond hair was pulled back into a neat bun. "Why don't you go ahead and have a seat?" she asked. "We're expecting two other families. We'll get started as soon as they get here."

Allie and her parents sat down at the middle of the room's three tables and quietly waited for the others to arrive. Finally, a tall, round woman walked in with her son, who was almost comically shorter than she was. "Melanie, so lovely to see you again," the woman boomed.

"Hello Mrs. Hanson, hello Boyd. Please have a seat." Melanie gestured to the Campbells. "This is Allie Campbell and her parents, Mr. and Mrs. Campbell."

"How very good to meet you," boomed Mrs. Hanson.

"Hi," said Boyd shyly. Allie guessed that Boyd was her age, perhaps a year younger. She smiled at him as he sat down at the table to the right of them.

Next, a girl who looked to be a few years older than Allie walked in. She was long and thin and swanlike. Her dad came in behind her. He was tall, too, and almost completely bald. Melanie introduced them as Amy and Mr. Fielding. The Fieldings quietly greeted the other families and took their seats to the Campbells' left.

With everyone seated, class got started. Melanie began by discussing which foods affect blood sugar: namely, foods with carbohydrates. Allie had already started learning how to count carbs, but it was helpful to find out exactly which foods fell into that category, and to better understand the reasons why they affected blood sugar so much.

Melanie went into detail about how to choose healthy foods, balance the amount of carbohydrate being eaten, read food labels for ingredients and carbohydrates, and more. She also taught the families how to measure and weigh the food they ate. She even had a little food scale.

Finally, Melanie talked about how to plan for meals and snacks. Allie wished she'd had this class before her friends went out for ice cream. Then she could have planned to work in a scoop of chocolate ice cream.

When the morning session was over, the families took a quick lunch break. They sat together outside, chatting casually and eating packed lunches. It turned out that both Boyd and Amy had been diagnosed right around the time Allie had. Boyd was shy, but nice; and Amy turned out to be very outgoing. Allie's previous classes had just been her and her parents, and it was nice to feel that there were other kids going through what she was. By the time they went back inside for the afternoon session, Allie felt a lot more comfortable just knowing that she was in good company.

The afternoon was spent talking about how physical activity and sports affected blood sugar. Amy was a dancer, and Boyd played baseball. Melanie talked to them about how activity, food, and insulin all need to be balanced. Allie learned that planning ahead for physical activity—like practice or a game—and working out a plan with her medical team was going to be important when she got back on the field. She also learned that it would take some time to understand all this and get it balanced.

Geez, this is a lot of info, Allie thought. But she was glad to be learning it. Hopefully, she could put it to good use and be back on the field in no time.

At the end of the afternoon, Allie and her family said good-bye to Amy and Boyd and their parents. The lessons and support from Melanie had made Allie feel more prepared than she had been before, more equipped to handle her diabetes. And getting to know Boyd and Amy made her feel like she wasn't alone in all this. That was a huge relief. Allie was feeling tougher and more confident than she had in a while.

"Well, Alligator," Mr. Campbell said as the family made their way back to the car. "You ready to go back to school tomorrow?"

And just like that, Allie's confidence deflated once more.

Chapter 4

It was Monday morning, and Allie was sitting at the kitchen table, mindlessly staring at the new medical ID bracelet that she and her mom had picked out and that she now wore on her left wrist. Allie couldn't help but feel like it pronounced her diabetes a little too loudly.

Allie's mom set a plate of breakfast in front of her, bringing her back to the present. Today would be Allie's first day back at school. School. Just thinking about going back made Allie feel nervous all over again. She had gone to see Dr. Cass for a follow-up appointment on Friday, and she had given Allie the all clear to go back to school. In fact, Dr. Cass seemed positively optimistic. If only Allie felt that way about heading back to class.

Allie and her parents had put together a pack of essentials that Allie would take with her to school. Inside, among other things, were her glucose meter to check her blood sugar during the day, extra lancets and test strips, and her logbook to keep track of her blood sugar. Allie's mom had stopped by the school on Friday to drop off Allie's insulin and syringes with the nurse. Her dad had gone to the grocery store the day before to stock up on a bunch of healthy snacks. He also bought some glucose tablets, which Allie could take if her blood sugar was low. She knew she was prepared, but managing her diabetes at school would be very different from doing it at home with her parents.

Allie quietly ate her breakfast. When she was done, she carried her plate to the sink, let out a deep sigh, and picked up her backpack. There was no more putting it off. The bus would be on the corner in just a few minutes.

The hallways of Chestnut Ridge Middle School were crowded and noisy, with students talking to one another, lockers slamming, and the occasional teacher walking past. Allie greeted a couple of classmates and headed for her locker.

She knew that, to everyone else, she seemed exactly the same as she was before her diagnosis. She certainly *looked* just the same. But she *felt* different, as though her diagnosis had made her a slightly different person. She supposed that, in a way, it had. Allie tried to shrug off the feeling, grabbing her science book off the top shelf of her locker and shoving it in her backpack.

On the way to class, Allie ran into Jo. Allie was relieved to see her best friend in the hallway—such a normal school-day occurrence—until she remembered she still hadn't told Jo about her diabetes.

"Hey!" Allie said, trying to make her voice as casual as possible.

"Hi, Al!" Jo exclaimed. "I'm so glad you're feeling better and back at school! Do you have a lot of work to catch up on?"

"I guess so." Allie shrugged her shoulders. "My mom brought some of my work home last week, but I still have to write that paper for English. Yuck."

"Oh, geez," Jo said. "Well, let me know if you need any help. By the way, did the doctors ever figure out why you were so

34

sick? Was it just a weird bug or something?"

Allie hesitated. She didn't want to lie, but she wasn't ready to tell her friend about her diabetes. "Yeah," she said. "Just a little bug . . . I guess they don't really know, must have been some kind of virus . . ." Allie sputtered out the rambling words. She was sure Jo would see right through her, but Jo just nodded.

"That's strange," Jo said skeptically. "Usually, the doctor can figure out what's wrong. Anyway, I'm just glad you're feeling better."

"Thanks," Allie said. "Well, hey . . . I've got to run to class. I'll see you later." Allie hurried off before Jo could protest. As she walked toward her class, she sighed. She knew she couldn't keep the secret from her best friend for long.

Allie could barely pay attention in class. She couldn't stop thinking about Jo, how she had lied to her face. She felt terrible.

She and Jo never kept secrets from each other.

But that wasn't the only thing that was distracting Allie. She was worried about her glucose level, too. Was it okay? What if something went wrong? She had checked her level this morning, and everything had been fine. But she still had three hours until lunchtime, when she would go visit the school nurse for her insulin shot. The day wasn't passing fast enough.

By the time second period rolled around, she couldn't take it anymore. Allie raised her hand.

"*Sí*, Allie?" her Spanish teacher, Mr. Nevins, asked.

"*¿Puedo ser excusada por favor?*" said Allie, asking in Spanish to be excused from class.

"*Sí*, okay," Mr. Nevins responded.

Allie stuffed her lancet and glucose meter in the pocket of her hoodie and grabbed the hall pass. She was glad her mom had arranged it so that she could go down to the nurse's office to check her blood sugar in private whenever she needed to.

The school nurse, Ms. Jacobs, was a round, middle-aged woman with a chin-length gray bob.

"Hi, Ms. Jacobs," Allie said, introducing herself. "I'm Allie Campbell."

"Oh, yes, I spoke with your mom on Friday," said Ms. Jacobs with a generous smile. "It's nice to meet you. How can I help you?"

"I just wanted to check my blood sugar," said Allie.

"Go right ahead," Ms. Jacobs said. "You can come on down anytime you'd like."

Allie took a reading and saw that her level was within target range. She immediately felt better. She thanked Ms. Jacobs and made her way back to class.

But that feeling of relief quickly disappeared as other worries took its place. As the morning went on, the homework Allie had missed continued to build up. She thought she had been in pretty good shape in terms of the work she'd missed, but she was starting to feel a little left behind in classes after missing so much school. Allie had never felt like she learned *that* much in a week, but suddenly it seemed as if every class had moved on without her.

The lunch bell rang, and Allie headed back to the nurse's office to test her blood sugar and get her shot.

"Hi again, Ms. Jacobs," Allie said. "I'm here for my insulin shot now."

"Oh, of course!" Ms. Jacobs said. "Why don't you have a seat over on that bench, next to the young man there. I'll be right with you."

Allie looked over to the bench and saw another eighth-grade boy she vaguely recognized. He had shaggy light brown hair and was reading a science fiction novel with a picture of a UFO on the front.

The boy looked up from his book. "Hi," he said.

"Hi," Allie said shyly.

"I have diabetes, too," he blurted.

A confused look passed over Allie's face.

"I overheard you telling Ms. Jacobs you're here for your shot," he explained quickly. "I didn't mean to eavesdrop."

"Oh, it's okay," Allie said, introducing herself.

"I'm Thomas," the boy said.

Before either of them could say anything else, Ms. Jacobs called Thomas over. He got up, swung his backpack over his shoulder, and brushed his hair out of his big blue eyes. "I come in here every day at lunch for my shot, so, uh, I'll probably see you around."

Allie gulped. "Bye."

She watched Thomas go behind the curtain with Ms. Jacobs. So she wasn't the only one in school with diabetes. That actually made her feel a bit better. Like maybe she wasn't so alone in this after all. Sure, she'd met the kids at the diabetes education class, but it wasn't like she'd ever really see them again. This was a kid her age, at her school, who was going through exactly what she was. She was comforted by the thought.

Finally, it was Allie's turn to go back and see Ms. Jacobs. Her palms were a little sweaty. She had never given herself an insulin shot without her parents around.

"You all right, sweetie?" Ms. Jacobs asked.

"I'm just kind of nervous," Allie said. "This is my first day back to school, and my mom and my diabetes team are the only people who have ever helped me give myself a shot."

Ms. Jacobs nodded. "I understand," she said. "If it makes you feel any better, I've been helping out kids with diabetes at this school for many, many years."

Allie smiled. That did make her feel a bit better.

Allie tested her blood sugar. Then Ms. Jacobs helped her figure out how much insulin to take, and Allie gave herself her shot. Before long, Ms. Jacobs sent her on her way.

"See you tomorrow, Allie," the nurse said with a wink.

Allie waved at Ms. Jacobs. "See you then," she said.

Chapter 5

By the time Allie walked into the cafeteria, her reusable lunch bag in hand, the room was swarming with sixth, seventh, and eighth graders all talking over one another.

Allie spotted Jo and her other soccer friends at their usual table. Nearly everyone from her travel team attended Chestnut Ridge Middle School, and they always lunched together.

"Allie! You're back at school!" the

ever-excited Marnie exclaimed when she saw Allie approach.

"Hi," Allie said, taking a seat at the table and setting her lunch bag in front of her.

"How come you're late?" Jo asked. Allie thought she caught something in Jo's eye—something that indicated suspicion. But it passed, and Allie figured Jo was just curious. After all, Allie usually prided herself on getting places on time.

"Oh," Allie paused, "I just had to talk to Mr. Nevins about my makeup assignment. No big deal."

Jo nodded, looking down at her food. "Gotcha."

"Are you going to be at soccer practice tomorrow night, then?" Charlene asked.

"Oh, yep! You bet," Allie said. It would be her first practice since her diagnosis. Allie's pulse quickened at the thought.

Allie noticed that her friends were all still

looking at her. Allie wasn't one for attention, and she didn't want them to ask any more questions about her being sick.

"So, what were you guys just talking about?" she asked, attempting to change the subject.

Her plan worked. The attention was diverted from her and back to the topic of the latest scary movie they wanted to see. For now.

Allie pulled out the contents of her lunch bag—a turkey and cheese sandwich, celery, an apple, and crackers. Allie usually ate pretty healthily, so thankfully her lunch wasn't much different from usual. Nothing to draw any attention to her.

As Allie bit into her sandwich, she caught Jo's eye. Her friend's gaze lingered on her for a minute, a slightly confused expression on her face. Allie looked away.

Jo clearly knew Allie was keeping something from her; she just didn't know what.

Chapter 6

That night after school, Coach Rebecca pulled up to Allie's house in her little red hybrid car. Allie's parents had invited her over to talk about Allie's diabetes — how it would affect her play, and what Coach Rebecca should know to help Allie be at her best.

When Allie answered the door, Coach Rebecca wrapped her in a big hug. "How are you doing, Al?" she asked, using Jo's nickname for her.

Allie hesitated for a moment. But there was something about Coach Rebecca's inviting smile that made Allie want to open up about her diabetes. Maybe it had something to do with trying to hide it all day at school.

"I'm okay," Allie said. "All of this diabetes stuff is hard to get used to."

"I'm sure it is," Coach Rebecca said comfortingly. "But you're a tough chick. You'll get through this just fine."

Allie smiled—her first genuine smile all day. Coach Rebecca had a way of making you feel like you could do anything, just by saying the simplest things. It was one of the reasons she was such a great coach.

Allie invited Coach Rebecca in. The two of them sat down on the couch, and Allie's parents joined them.

"Well, I sure am glad you're coming back to play with us again, Allie," Coach Rebecca said. "We're going to need you if we want to make it to the league championship. I think you might just be our good-luck charm." Coach Rebecca winked.

"Thanks, Coach," Allie said. "But . . ." Allie had thought long and hard about what she was about to say, but it was hard to make herself form the words. ". . . Are you sure you still want me as a starter? I mean, I've been out for more than a week. Are you sure—"

"Allie," Coach Rebecca said kindly. "You're the only one I want playing center mid. Got it? You're a rock star. It's time you had your chance to shine on the Tornados!"

Allie gave Coach Rebecca a small smile. "Thanks," she said. "I hope you're right. I'm pretty nervous about this weekend's game."

"Don't even worry about it," Coach Rebecca said. "You've got enough to worry about with your diabetes and your schoolwork and everything else. Soccer is supposed to be fun! I just want you to go out there on

Saturday and have a good time, okay?"

"Okay," Allie said.

"So, what can I do to help you out tomor-row when you come back and join us?" Coach Rebecca asked.

Allie and her parents explained to Coach Rebecca what her diagnosis meant for play-ing soccer. Allie also explained that she would have to check her blood sugar before, during, and after every practice, and if she wasn't feeling well.

"Got it," Coach Rebecca said. "Is there some sort of sign you want to give me in case you need to come off the field and check your blood sugar?"

Allie thought for a moment. "Sure," she said. "How about if I do something simple, like wave at you?"

"Works for me!" Coach Rebecca said.

"We have supplies for you in case Allie's blood sugar gets low," Mrs. Campbell said, holding up a small bag. Allie and her parents went through the contents of the bag, showing Coach Rebecca what everything was and how to use it.

"Sounds good," Coach Rebecca said, scratching her cheek thoughtfully. "Allie, have you given any thought to telling the others on the team?"

Allie looked down. "I actually wanted to talk to you about that," she said. "It's not that my diabetes is a secret, exactly, but I don't want them to know just yet."

"Are you sure?" Coach Rebecca asked. "I'm certain they'll understand."

"I'm sure," Allie said.

"Okay," Coach Rebecca said. "But since you've missed a few practices and sat out the last game, they probably know that something's up."

"I know," Allie said. "I'll tell them. When I'm ready."

Chapter 7

The next afternoon, Allie was back at soccer practice. It had been another long day at school, and although she wanted to get back out there and play soccer, she wasn't sure she was ready yet. But her parents had given her some words of gentle encouragement.

"If you're really not feeling up to it, you can wait another week to get back to practice," her mom had said. "Everyone will understand. But just remember that it's good for you to get out there and play."

"I think it will make you feel a lot better to spend some time with your friends," her dad had added. "But it's your choice."

Allie knew that her parents were right, and she tried to shake off her worries. She just hoped nothing went wrong with her blood sugar while she was out on the field. She had worn a long-sleeved T-shirt to cover up her diabetes ID bracelet, hoping to prevent any questions that might reveal what was wrong.

"All right, girls, let's scrimmage!" Coach Rebecca said, breaking the girls off into two teams. Allie and Jo were on opposing sides. The girls lined up to play. Coach Rebecca blew the whistle and the game started.

Jo dribbled the ball through Allie's team's forwards and midfielders. Helen, who was on Allie's scrimmage team, stole the ball from Jo and looked for someone to pass to.

"I'm open! I'm open!" Becky Davis, the left midfielder, yelled. Helen passed the ball to Becky, but she was quickly boxed in by Charlene. Becky got rid of the ball, passing it to Allie.

But Allie completely missed the pass. Jo stole the ball and blew right past Allie to score a goal.

Allie turned beet red. "I'm sorry," she said.

She had to focus. But all she could think about was her blood sugar level.

Allie waved her arm at Coach Rebecca — their agreed-upon signal — who nodded for her to come off the field.

"Aisha, why don't you fill in for Allie for a minute," Coach Rebecca said. Allie saw Aisha roll her eyes. Allie's mouth fell open in shock at Aisha's reaction. Then she remembered what she was doing and grabbed her blood sugar meter out of her bag.

"I'm just going to run inside, Coach," she said. She wanted to check her level in private, so none of her teammates would know what she was doing.

Allie headed for the middle school, making her way back to the nurse's office. Ms. Jacobs stayed late after school in order to accommodate kids who might need medical attention during practice. Allie greeted Ms. Jacobs, then took a finger prick. She held her finger up to the meter and saw that her blood sugar was fine.

Feeling somewhat relieved, Allie headed back out to the field. She had a drink of water on the sideline, rested for a couple of minutes, and then rejoined the girls.

Allie tried to get her head back into the game, but she just wasn't comfortable. She was distracted and kept missing passes and falling behind. Finally, she decided to take another break to make sure that her sugar was all right. This would be the last time this practice, she promised herself.

"Are you feeling all right?" Coach Rebecca asked Allie.

"I think so," she said. "I just wanted to check my blood sugar to make sure I'm okay."

"You just checked it about fifteen minutes ago, right?" Coach Rebecca asked her quietly. "Is everything okay?"

"I'm just worried," Allie said. "What if I didn't check it right? What if something goes wrong?"

"This will be easier once you get the hang of it. But if you feel uncomfortable and want to double-check, you should go ahead," Coach Rebecca said.

"Thanks, Coach," Allie said. "You're right. I think I'm okay. I don't feel low."

"Just remember, I spoke to your parents

and know exactly what to do if anything goes wrong."

Allie wanted to believe her. But playing soccer with diabetes was going to take some getting used to.

Chapter 8

After another tough practice, Saturday's game arrived. The Tornados were playing the Fairfield Flyers—Julie's new team. Allie was going up against the girl who used to play her position.

By the time the first half drew to a close, Allie had begun to doubt that the Tornados could take the Flyers. The game was neck and neck, with the score tied at 3–3. Allie certainly didn't feel like she was bringing her A-game. The rest of the Tornados were playing their hardest, sweating in the chilly sixty-degree mid-September afternoon. But the Flyers, in their bright yellow jerseys, were a tough bunch of girls.

Julie was no exception. She was the kind of player you wanted on your *own* team, not the opposing one, Allie thought. It was strange to be competing against a friend. She and Julie had been battling it out all game, and Allie had to admit to herself that, at the end of the day, perhaps Julie was just a better player.

Allie had been working her hardest to keep up, but she couldn't shake the feelings that had been dogging her at practice all week. Was her blood sugar okay? Should she take a break to check it? She just felt so unsure of herself.

The referee blew the whistle to signify the end of the first half, and the team gathered around Coach Rebecca for halftime.

"You guys can do this!" she said. "You've had so many shots on goal. Just don't back down. Keep up the good work out there, okay?"

The team rallied together in a circle and put their hands in the middle. "'Let's go, Tornados,' at the count of three," Coach Rebecca said. "One, two, three!"

"LET'S GO, TORNADOS!" the girls shouted.

The Tornados headed back out onto the field. But before Allie could join the rest of the team, Coach Rebecca pulled her aside.

"You okay out there, kiddo?" she asked. "You seem like you're holding back a little bit."

"I'm okay," Allie said, taking a swig from her water bottle. "Just nerves, I guess."

"All right," Coach Rebecca said. "You just let me know if you need to sit out for a few minutes."

"I'm going to run inside and check my blood sugar okay? I'll be back in just a minute."

"Sure thing," said Coach Rebecca. "Whatever you need."

Allie used her blood glucose meter inside the soccer shed's bathroom. Everything was fine. She ate a snack because she knew she had the rest of the game to play. Then she got back out on the field. But the rest of the game continued to be rough for her—and for the rest of her team. The Tornados fought tooth and nail, but they couldn't get another goal. And Allie wasn't much help. She just didn't feel her usual confident self. When Julie ran up the field to score on the Tornados' goal, Allie was helpless to stop her.

In the end, the Flyers edged out the Tornados by a single point—the Tornados' first loss of the season. Their record was three wins and one loss. They'd have to step it up in the remaining two games of the season in order to make the league championship.

As was tradition after each game, the two teams stood in single-file lines facing each other. The opposing teams walked by each other, high-fiving each player as they passed. "Good game," Allie told the other girls, even though it hadn't been — especially not for her.

Finally, Allie reached Julie. The two girls shared a hug. Allie certainly couldn't fault her friend for winning.

"Great job out there, Jules," Allie said. "We miss you so much."

"I miss you, too!" Julie said. "That was a tough game. It was a little weird playing against you guys, I have to say. Part of me was rooting for your team, if you can believe it."

Allie smiled. "Thanks," she said. "You totally deserved that win, though."

"Keep up the good work," Julie said. "You guys have a great team."

The girls chatted for a couple more minutes, then said good-bye. Allie couldn't help but notice that Julie hadn't complimented her playing skills in return. But she could hardly hold it against her. Allie knew she had been off her game today.

As Allie headed back to the sidelines, feeling a little defeated, Aisha and Helen walked by her.

"Where *were* you today, Allie?" asked Aisha in a sarcastic tone.

Allie looked to the ground, her face red. She had done her best. Wasn't that enough?

"Aisha!" Helen reprimanded, elbowing her friend in the side. "Don't listen to her, Allie. It was a tough game today, for everyone."

Allie climbed into the backseat of her parents' car after the game and rested her head on the cool glass of the car window. She felt crummy about the loss, and wondered when she'd be able to play like normal again. She knew the problem was in her head, not in her body. Allie closed her eyes and sighed.

"You okay, sweetie?" her dad asked.

"Yeah," Allie said. "I just wish I had played better."

"Are you kidding? You did great!" said Allie's mom. "This is your first game back and you still managed to start a game *and* play the whole way through!"

"Your mom's right," said Mr. Campbell. "We're proud of you."

Allie gave her parents a small smile. "Thanks, guys," she said. But Allie was her own harshest critic. She wanted to pick up the pace and help her team get to the league championship. She knew she had to step it up.

Chapter 9

After the game, Allie showered, put on her favorite comfy jeans and a cozy sweater, and fixed her long, wavy blond hair.

That night was Charlene's birthday sleepover. Allie's parents weren't sure they were comfortable with her spending the night away from home so soon after her diagnosis, and frankly, Allie felt the same way. So Allie was going to leave after presents were opened.

Allie had told Charlene and her friends that she had to be somewhere early the next morning—"a family thing," she said. She hated lying about it. What was diabetes *doing* to her? Allie had always been an honest person. But bending the truth was the only way she could see to keep her diabetes to herself.

Suddenly Allie heard a car pull up. Jo and her dad were bringing Allie to the sleepover.

"Hey, Al!" said Jo. She was sitting in the front seat, wearing a sweater dress and leggings, Charlene's prettily wrapped birthday present on her lap. Her long, dark brown hair was twisted into a bun on the top of her head. The two girls chatted excitedly the whole ride over.

Jo's dad dropped them off at Charlene's house, and Allie and Jo skipped up to the front porch. Jo rang the doorbell.

"Hey, ladies!" Charlene shouted when

she opened the door. Charlene had dressed up for the occasion, wearing a cute navy blue pleated skirt with a belted cardigan on top and a pair of patterned tights. She had even added a bit of silver eye shadow to her almond-shaped eyes.

"Happy birthday!" said Allie and Jo in unison.

"Thanks!" Charlene said. "Come on in."

Charlene's house was one of those cozy, country-style houses filled with comfy furniture and interesting knickknacks all over the place. Allie immediately felt right at home. She was starting to have second thoughts about going home early. Maybe she could manage here just fine for the night. After all, Charlene's parents were around and could help Allie out if she needed it. But that would mean spending a night away from her parents. Allie wasn't sure she was ready for that yet.

Charlene led Allie and Jo down to the basement, which was decorated with balloons and streamers. An entire corner was filled with overnight bags, sleeping bags, and pillows. An old card table covered in a colorful tablecloth held gifts from the girls. Allie added hers to the pile and joined Aisha and Becky on the huge wraparound couch. Jacqui and Jenni Hill, who both played defense, were on the couch, too. Marnie and Helen sat in armchairs across from them.

"Hey, Allie! Hey, Jo!" Helen greeted them, her pixie cut enhanced by a sparkly head-band.

Just as the girls were settling in, the door-bell rang.

"Pizza's here!" Charlene said. The girls raced upstairs to eat.

Allie couldn't wait to eat a slice of pizza! Her dad had called Charlene's mom ear-lier in the week to find out what was on the menu. Then Allie and her dietitian had worked out a meal plan and an adjustment to her insulin dosage to allow Allie to eat what was being served at the party. Allie was still getting used to counting carbohydrates and was glad the diabetes center was available to help her out. She excused herself to the kitchen, where Charlene's mom got out her insulin for her, and Allie took her shot.

Allie joined the other girls in the dining room. She grabbed a slice of pizza, a giant helping of salad, and a diet soda.

"Well, today's game stunk," said Charlene, "but having you girls over to celebrate my birthday makes my day all better." Charlene looked at all of her friends with a beaming smile on her face.

"Hear, hear!" said Marnie, raising her drink.

Jo lifted her soda. "I'll drink to that!" she said.

The girls laughed, lifting their soda cans and clanking them together.

"You know," said Helen, "I feel like we did all right out there. Maybe if we had practiced a little harder, we could have taken them. Maybe we just needed today to gel as a team with our amazing new starter, Allie." Helen winked at Allie.

Allie blushed. Helen *looked* like she was being genuine, but Allie was sure she was just being nice.

Before she could respond, Allie heard a snort. It was Aisha. When Aisha realized she was the only one who had reacted to Helen's comment, she quickly wiped the smug look off her face.

The other girls pretended not to notice Aisha's reaction. Allie brushed it off as best she could, and turned back to Helen. "Thanks," she said. "Hopefully next week is even better."

"Can you believe we've only got two weeks until the league championship game, if we can get ourselves there?" Jo asked, changing the subject. "Our record is still pretty great. There's only one other team with a single loss, and that's the Fairfield Flyers."

"Julie sure did pick a good team to join!" said Marnie.

"No kidding," Charlene replied.

"Well, hopefully we'll get another win this coming weekend," Helen said.

"I hope so!" Jo answered.

Allie tried her best to be enthusiastic, but Aisha's negative interjection was really getting to her. Sure, Allie hadn't played her best that day. She had a lot going on mentally that kept her from focusing. But deep down, she knew she was a good player. The more Allie thought about it, the more she knew that she had it in her to be an awesome center midfielder. Just thinking about it brought back

some of the confidence Allie had been missing since her diagnosis. She wanted to prove
Aisha wrong, to show her team that she was
meant to play this position.

Allie knew that Aisha wanted her spot, but
she couldn't understand why she was acting as though she didn't like Allie. It wasn't
like she'd done anything to her personally.
Even if Aisha *was* acting silly, Allie hated
for a member of her team to dislike her. She
hoped that, with time, the two could become
friends. Though at the moment, it seemed
kind of doubtful.

After dinner, Charlene opened her presents. All too soon it was time for Allie to go
home. Her teammates all hugged her good-
bye.

"I don't get why you can't stay! You're
going to miss one killer game of truth or
dare. . . ." Marnie said in her most enticing
voice.

"Are you *sure* you can't just stay and get up *really* early tomorrow morning?" Charlene asked.

Allie shrugged. "Wish I could," she said. "But you know my parents . . . once they have their minds made up, they stick to it!" Allie bit the inside of her cheek to push back her feelings of guilt about lying to her friends.

"We'll miss you!" Helen said.

"Have fun, guys," Allie said, heading out the door.

Her friends waved as Allie walked down the moonlit sidewalk to her parents' car, which sat idling in the driveway.

Chapter 10

By the following week, Allie was playing a little better. But she still couldn't fully help being distracted by thoughts of her blood glucose level. It was so frustrating! She should have control over her mind, not let it control her!

Jo sensed Allie's frustration and approached her after practice.

"Hey," she said, a concerned smile on her face.

"Hi," Allie answered, looking down at the ground.

"Look, what's going on?" Jo asked, trying to search her friend's expression. "I know something's the matter. You haven't been acting yourself these last couple of weeks, ever since you were out sick. I'm worried about you."

"No, I'm not—" Allie started. "It's just that I . . . I'm going through a lot right now."

"You are?" said Jo. "Like what? I'm your best friend. The one person who will be there for you no matter what. Don't you know that you can tell me anything?"

"It's just . . . you wouldn't understand," Allie said.

A hurt expression crossed Jo's face. Allie felt terrible. She certainly never meant to make her friend feel like she didn't trust her.

Jo took a deep breath and looked at Allie. "All right," she said. "I'm not going to push you about this. Just know that I'm here whenever you need me, okay?"

Allie nodded. "I know," she said.

Jo turned and walked away. Allie felt like she'd been coping with her diabetes better. Her soccer skills were coming back. School was finally not a complete hassle, what with having to visit the nurse's office each day and all. But now Allie felt worse than ever. All her best friend wanted was to be there for her, and Allie couldn't give her that. She had been a terrible friend, keeping a huge secret like this from Jo. What was she so worried about, anyway? Why was she so afraid of Jo's reaction? She couldn't put her finger on it. It was like Allie was still in denial about her diabetes herself, and telling Jo would make it real.

Everyone who knew about her diabetes kept telling Allie that everything would be okay. So how come nothing *felt* okay right now?

* * *

Allie went home from practice and shut herself in her bedroom. She laid facedown on her bed and began to cry.

She felt completely helpless. Nothing was as easy as it had been before. Wasn't eighth grade hard enough without the problems of having diabetes?

And now Allie had hurt Jo, her best friend in the world, something she had never meant to do.

Finally, Allie stopped crying. She wiped her eyes. She couldn't take this anymore. She needed to call her friend.

Jo picked up on the third ring.

"What are you up to?" Allie asked.

"Nothing much; just studying," Jo replied.

"Can I come over?" Allie asked. "I need to talk."

Jo sounded elated. "Of course!" she said.

* * *

Jo opened the door and welcomed her best friend inside. As always, Jo's house smelled like vanilla candles and warm cookies.

Jo led Allie up to her room. The walls were covered in posters, and knickknacks, pictures, and soccer trophies took up every inch of space. The cheerful, cluttered space matched Jo's personality perfectly.

The two girls plopped down on her bed, which was covered with a frilly purple bedspread. Allie picked up one of Jo's teddy bears and put it in her lap.

"So, what's going on?" Jo asked.

"Well," Allie said, "I wasn't really sick with a mystery illness last week."

"I kind of had a feeling," Jo said. "You're a terrible liar."

Allie laughed. "I know," she said. Then her face got serious. She took a deep breath, readying herself to spill the beans. "What really happened was that I found out I have type 1 diabetes."

The smile fell from Jo's face. "Oh, gosh," she said.

"I'm really sorry I didn't tell you sooner," Allie replied.

"Oh, Al, I'm so sorry!" Jo said. "Are you okay?"

Allie thought about it. "I'm learning to manage my diabetes," she said. "I have to go to all these classes to learn about diabetes, and I have to take insulin shots every day and watch what I eat," Allie said.

"You have to take shots *every day*?" Jo asked.

"Yup, four of them," Allie said, nodding.

"But you don't even like needles!"

"I'm much better with them now. I kind of have to be. I guess you get used to them."

"Wow," Jo said. "Why did you decide to keep this a secret?"

"I don't know," Allie said. "Part of me

wasn't ready to deal with having diabetes myself. I didn't know how to tell anyone else." Allie bit her lip. "I guess I was also worried that people would think I was weird, having to give myself shots all the time. I didn't want anyone to treat me differently."

"Oh, Allie!" Jo said. "You will always be my best friend, no matter what. I wouldn't care if I found out you were an alien. You'd still be the same person!"

"I know that now," Allie said, nodding. "I still don't know if I'm ready to tell the rest of the team, though," she said.

"They know something's going on," Jo told Allie. "Everyone's been asking me if I know what's wrong. Even Aisha."

"Really?" Allie asked, shocked.

"Yep," Jo said. "I've just been telling them I don't know. Which was the truth. Anyway, tell them whenever you're ready. Just know that they totally have your back, just like me."

Chapter 11

That Saturday, Allie's mom and dad drove her and Jo to their game. On the half-hour car ride to Doonsville—where their opponents, the Doonsville Dragons, were from— the sky opened up and it began to pour.

Allie still hadn't told the rest of her teammates about her diabetes, but she felt a million times better now that her best friend knew what was troubling her. The butterflies Allie had felt last game no longer tormented her. This time, she felt ready to play tough.

As the minivan pulled up the dirt drive to the fields, Allie could see the puddles already starting to form on the grassy terrain. Her teammates, wearing their Kelly green jerseys, were huddled under umbrellas on the sidelines, waiting for everyone to arrive so they could begin warming up.

"Allie! Jo!" called Marnie, seeing them arrive.

"Hey, guys!" Allie said. Seeing her teammates smiling at her was like seeing the sun peering through the clouds. Allie's mood lifted even more. What had she been so nervous about before, anyway? Handling her diabetes during practice had gotten easier, and she had her best friend on her side. Today was her day to shine!

The rain lightened up a little bit as Allie and her teammates warmed up on one end of the field. On the opposite end, the Dragons ran drills of their own, their bright orange jerseys standing out against the gloomy weather.

By the time the girls got into their starting positions, their hair was slick with rain, their shin guards and jerseys spattered with mud.

Allie stood at center field, observing the opposing team while she waited for the whistle. She spotted the Dragons' center midfielder. The girl was compact and muscular, with a tough-looking expression on her face. Allie steeled herself. She was ready for this. There was no reason to be intimidated.

The ref blew the whistle, and the game began. Jo and Sydney Conway, another Tornados forward, took off with the ball. Allie stayed close behind, ready to do her part.

The Dragons' center midfielder tackled Jo for the ball, deftly stealing it away.

Allie braced herself as the girl barreled toward her. Before Allie could stop her, the girl passed the ball off to another teammate, leaving Allie in the dust. But Allie wasn't about to let one little mishap get her down. This would *not* be a repeat of last week's game!

Minutes later, the Dragons' forward charged the goal. Marnie easily stole the ball away, passing it back to Allie. In a flash, Allie was up the field. The Dragons' midfielder was on her tail. It took all the energy Allie could muster, but she managed to stay ahead. Allie spotted Jo just in front of her and quickly passed the ball ahead. In the blink of an eye, Jo scored.

The sidelines erupted. Allie leaped into the air. She had just made her first assist as a starter!

Becky hugged Allie. "Nice job!" she shouted as the team lined up again.

"Thanks!" Allie panted, a beaming smile breaking out across her face.

The rest of the game went by in a blur. Allie raced up and down the field, assisting the defenders and passing the ball up to the forwards as often as she could. Halftime came and went. Allie went inside to check her level, and everything looked fine. Her confidence back in full force, Allie put her diabetes out of her mind and focused on the game. Pure adrenaline carried her along, and she continued to outpace the Dragons' center midfielder throughout the second half.

Before Allie knew it, Jo and the other forwards had put up four goals. The other team hadn't even scored once! The game was over. The Tornados now had a 4–1 record for the season.

"Good game, Allie!" Marnie said, patting her on the back. "You played like a rock star!"

Back on the sidelines, Allie caught up to Aisha. She hoped she could clear the air between them.

"Hey, nice job today," Allie told her. But Aisha didn't say anything. She just gave Allie a little half smile, grabbed her things, and walked off.

But Allie didn't have time to dwell on it. Jo tackled her in a hug from behind. "I knew you could do that," she said, keeping her voice quiet. "Diabetes or no diabetes, my best friend is an *awesome* soccer player!"

Allie laughed. "I wouldn't even be here if it weren't for you!" she said.

Allie felt awesome—exhilarated, even. She felt like she belonged here, on the field.

"Come on, Allie!" Jo called. Allie jogged off after her friend for a celebratory team cheer.

Chapter 12

At practice on Thursday, Allie warmed up with the rest of the team. She was still riding high from the win on Saturday, but for some reason, she couldn't relax. Something was nagging at her, and she knew what it was. It was high time she told her teammates about her diabetes. *I can put it off for a little while longer,* Allie told herself, trying to focus on her drills.

At the end of practice, Coach Rebecca gathered the girls around for a pep talk, rallying the troops for their big game on Saturday.

"All right, ladies," she said. "I've had a look at the other teams' records, and we're still in the running for the league championship. We're one win away from getting ourselves there, but we've got to beat the Greenstown Tigers on Saturday. I've been so proud of you girls all season," she said, catching Allie's eye as she said this. "I know you've got what it takes. So rest up Friday night, and I'll see you on the field Saturday morning!"

After Coach Rebecca finished her talk, the girls milled around in the circle for a minute, waiting for their parents to pick them up.

This is the time, Allie thought. *Go on and tell them*, she encouraged herself.

Allie cleared her throat. "Hey, guys?" she said.

The girls all turned to look at Allie.

"What's up?" Marnie asked.

Allie took a deep breath, steeling herself. "There's something I want to tell you," she said.

Allie caught Coach Rebecca's eye again. She gave Allie an encouraging smile.

"I found out a couple of weeks ago that I have type 1 diabetes," she said. "I just wanted to let you all know. That's the real reason why I was gone from practice and school."

For a moment, no one said anything. Allie suddenly felt very uncomfortable. What were her friends thinking? Did they think she was some kind of weirdo? She was starting to regret having said anything, when suddenly, Marnie broke the silence.

"Oh, gosh," Marnie said. She walked up and hugged Allie. "You poor thing!"

"Is it serious?" Aisha asked, looking concerned. Allie tried not to let Aisha's sudden interest take her by surprise.

"It's manageable," Allie said. "I have to

give myself insulin shots, and I have to check my blood sugar and watch what I eat."

The girls had so many questions for Allie. They sat down in a circle on the grass, right in the middle of the field, and Allie told them all about her diabetes.

"We knew something was going on," Charlene said. "We're just glad you're okay."

"We were worried about you, but we didn't want to say anything because it seemed like maybe you weren't ready to tell us yet," Becky added.

"My cousin has type 1 diabetes," Helen said. "He's an eighth grader at our school. His name's Thomas Simons. He found out about a year ago."

"Thomas?" Allie asked. "Does he see the school nurse, too?"

"I think so," Helen said. "Why?"

"I know him," Allie said. "We both go to the nurse's office at lunchtime."

"Oh, cool!" Helen said. "Yeah, he's a real sweetie. I remember when he was diagnosed, he was super bummed out and it took him a while to start doing any of his sports again. He was super into outdoors stuff, like mountain biking and rock climbing, and he was afraid to go back to them. But now he's back out there doing it all."

If her friends' support hadn't lifted her spirits high enough, Helen's story made Allie feel even better, and more hopeful.

Life might never be exactly the same living with diabetes, but people did it all the time. Allie could still be Allie, diabetes and all.

"I think you deserve a group hug," Marnie said, smiling.

All the girls closed in around Allie, squeezing her tight. Tears rose to Allie's eyes. But this time, they were tears of happiness. How lucky she felt to have so many friends to help her through this.

Chapter 13

Allie nervously wrung her hands as she waited for the referee to blow his whistle, signifying the start of the game. She took a few deep breaths. This was the big one! If they beat the Tigers, they'd be in the championship game!

Calm down, Allie told herself. *You can do this.*

The game got off to a rocky start, with the Tigers dominating the field. Their offense was tough to keep up with. Before the Tornados knew what hit them, the Tigers had three shots on goal. Luckily, Marnie was able to stop every one of them. But the Tornados couldn't bank on Marnie alone.

"Allie, stay on their center mid!" Coach Rebecca called, reminding Allie to guard her counterpart on the opposing team.

Allie wasn't quite comfortable in the game yet. Her pace was slightly slower than usual, and she wasn't playing very aggressively. Did it have something to do with her blood sugar? She was probably just psyching herself out. Besides, she had checked it before the game and had a snack, too. Even if her level *did* drop, she knew how to take care of it. Allie tried her best to put any thoughts of her diabetes out of her mind, to focus on the game. She knew she could do this. She'd proven it last week with that awesome assist!

By halftime, the Tigers had put up one point. The Tornados—none.

"Come on girls, let's do this!" Coach Rebecca told them. "Their defense is weak, so let's attack them with all we've got! Forwards, keep doing what you're doing. Midfielders, I want you to help out the defense — keep those Tigers out of our end of the field. Defense, keep up the good work. Let's get 'em!"

Allie checked her blood sugar again, and everything looked fine. As the girls made their way back out to the field for the second half, Jo put her arm around her best friend.

"How are you doing out there?" she said.

"Okay," said Allie. "Just trying to get my head in the game."

"You can do it," Jo said. "We all believe in you."

Allie took Jo's words to heart. As the game got back under way, Allie started to believe in herself, too. She took a deep breath, mustered all her confidence, and attacked the field.

As the second half went on, Allie got more and more into the flow of the game, and as she did, she continued to gain self-assurance. Before she knew it, Allie had gotten possession of the ball, dodged the other team's defenses, and passed the ball up to Charlene, who sailed the ball into the net.

The Tornados and their fans erupted into cheers.

"Go, Allie! Nice pass!"

Allie turned to the sideline to see her mom and dad up on their feet in the stands, cheering their daughter on.

"Great work, Allie!" Coach Rebecca shouted.

Allie smiled.

By the middle of the second half, all of Allie's worries about her diabetes had escaped her mind. She ran up and down the field, playing like her old, confident self. She helped her defenders. She tackled the other team for the ball. She sped up the field and passed the ball to her forwards. With the full support of her parents, her teammates, and her coach, Allie felt like she couldn't lose. Nothing could stop her now!

Finally, toward the end of the half, the Tornados scored another goal. The game was over, and the Tornados had won, 3–2.

They were going to the league championship!

Chapter 14

"All right, girls," Coach Rebecca said at practice on Tuesday. "I want you to take it easy this week. Save up your energy for the big game." The Tornados would be facing the Fairfield Flyers—Julie's team—for the league trophy on Saturday.

Coach Rebecca split the girls up into two scrimmage teams for a casual game.

Allie was out on the field when she started to feel a little light-headed. She looked down at her hands and saw that they were shaking. She took a deep breath. This felt like the time she had experienced her first low at home. She had to get off the field and find out if something was wrong.

She calmly waved her right arm at Coach Rebecca, who nodded for Allie to come off the field.

"You feeling all right, Al?" she asked.

"Just a little woozy," Allie said, sitting down next to her soccer bag. She pulled out her glucose meter and took a reading.

"My blood sugar is low," Allie told Coach Rebecca. "I think I'm okay. I just need a few glucose tablets."

"Okay," Coach Rebecca said. "Take your time. Just let me know if you need anything else."

Her hands still shaking, Allie reached into her bag and grabbed the glucose tablets she had packed for just such an occasion. She took them, and after a little while she noticed that her hands had stopped shaking and the dizziness had passed.

Allie sighed. Moments like these were frustrating. She knew they were sure to happen from here on out, but she was glad she was beginning to learn what to expect when they did. She was getting to know her body better, learning to recognize the symptoms of high and low blood sugar and when she had to check her level.

Allie waited fifteen minutes and then checked her blood sugar again. It was fine, so she grabbed a quick snack, since she had the rest of the game to play, and jogged back onto the field.

"My glucose level was low," she explained to Becky.

"What does that mean?" Becky asked. Allie gladly explained.

Her teammates had been incredibly supportive. Instead of acting like Allie didn't have diabetes, they asked a lot of questions about it.

The more Allie was able to share about her diabetes with her friends, the better she felt. Just talking about her diabetes made her feel like a normal eighth grader again.

Since telling her friends about her diabetes, and since playing so well at last week's game, Allie's confidence had continued to grow. Even though the Flyers had bested the Tornados a few weeks back, Allie reminded herself that things had changed since then. She was learning to focus on the game, not on her diabetes. And the Tornados were playing as a team, all with the same goal in mind: to win the game on Saturday.

At practice on Thursday, Coach Rebecca paired Allie up with Aisha for a passing drill.

Aisha hadn't said or done anything rude to Allie since she had told the girls about her diabetes. In fact, Aisha had even been shyly smiling at Allie on occasion—a huge improvement from before. But Allie still felt awkward around her.

The two girls passed the ball back and forth, neither one really talking to the other. The quiet was just starting to get to Allie when Aisha spoke.

"Hey, Allie?" she said.

Allie kicked the ball back to Aisha and looked up. "Yeah?" she asked.

"I just wanted to say I'm sorry . . . for being kind of nasty to you before," she said.

"Oh," Allie said. She felt her cheeks flush. "It's, uh, it's okay."

"No, it's not," Aisha said. "I was totally jealous of you because I wanted to play center mid. You probably figured that out. But it's not your fault Coach Rebecca picked you to take over for Julie when she left."

Allie couldn't believe this was spilling out all of a sudden.

"Also, I'm sorry I was mean to you when

you were sick," she went on. "I didn't know that was why you weren't playing well. Not that that makes it okay. I should never have said anything like that to you."

"I'm not mad anymore," Allie said. "Actually, I was never really mad to begin with. I just didn't understand why you didn't like me."

"Didn't like you?" Aisha asked. "No, I think you're really nice. That made it harder to be upset about you taking my position." Aisha laughed. So did Allie. Aisha wasn't so bad after all, once you got to know her.

"I have an idea," Allie said. "Why don't I talk to Coach Rebecca? Maybe you and I can switch off positions from time to time. I love doing throw-ins, and I never get to do them playing center mid."

Aisha looked surprised. "You would do that?" she asked.

"Sure!" said Allie. "That's what teammates are for!"

Chapter 15

It was a Saturday in early October, and the air outside was cold. Leaves were falling from the tree outside Allie's window. But the sun was shining bright in a clear blue sky.

Allie woke up early, beating her alarm clock to the punch, and hopped right out of bed. Finally, the big day was here; the league championship game against the Fairfield Flyers.

Allie had written Julie an e-mail last night

to wish her and her team good luck. She was looking forward to seeing her friend again, but it was going to be a tough game.

Allie gave herself her insulin shot and followed it with a breakfast of milk, eggs, and toast, with some fresh fruit. Then she got ready, pulling on her Kelly green uniform, her shin guards and socks, and her cleats. She tied her long, wavy hair back into a tight ponytail and began to pack her bag with everything she would need for the game.

At her last meeting with her diabetes team, Allie and her nurse had worked out a game plan for how to manage her diabetes during the game. Each soccer game was sixty minutes of play time. Allie packed her blood glucose meter and enough testing supplies to get through the game. She also packed snacks to help keep her blood sugar from dropping too low, and glucose tablets and some juice just in case it did.

Whether they won or lost, the team was going to celebrate with a banquet after the game. They were all going to Coach Rebecca's house to commemorate a great season together. Allie had asked Coach Rebecca what food would be served so that she could figure out the amount of carbohydrate in the foods she'd be eating. There was going to be a celebratory cake and ice cream, and Allie definitely wanted some! She and her mom had worked with her diabetes team to figure out her insulin dosage based on her blood sugar and what she would eat. She'd be doing a lot of exercise before the banquet, and it was important that she factor that in, too.

Allie had a late-morning snack. Finally, she was ready to go. She felt energized and excited, and perhaps most importantly, she felt prepared.

She got in her parents' minivan, lugging her soccer bag along with her. Her parents drove her to the game, chatting the whole way.

"I can't believe it's already the end of the season!" Allie's mom said.

"Are you nervous, Alligator?" her dad asked.

"No, I feel pretty good!" Allie replied.

"Well, that's a good thing," Mr. Campbell said. "The Fairfield Flyers were tough competition the last time."

"Oh, Allie and the girls will be great, don't you think, Allie?"

"Of course, Mom," Allie said. *They sound more nervous than I am*, Allie thought, smiling to herself.

When Allie finally arrived at the field, she joined her teammates to warm up. She spotted Julie on the other side of the field and gave a friendly wave. Eventually, Coach Rebecca called the whole team over for a pregame pep talk.

"All right," she said. "Everybody gather 'round. You guys have worked so hard all season. We've been through a lot together, and whether we win or lose this game, no one can take that away from us. What I want you girls to do is go out there and give it your all. Show them that you are not the same team they played a few weeks back. You've learned to play together, and you are stronger now than you ever were. Now, go get 'em!"

The girls cheered and jogged out onto the field to take their positions.

As the game got under way, it became clear that the Flyers were up against more than they'd bargained for.

The Tornados played their hearts out, and Allie was no exception. For the first half, she started out at right midfield while Aisha played center mid. Allie found herself enjoying the new position. When the opposing team kicked the ball out of bounds, Allie got to pick it up from the sidelines and toss it back in to her teammates. She quickly discovered she was pretty good at that, too.

In the middle of the first half the score was still 0–0. By halftime, each team had scored a goal. Allie checked her level again and found that it was still where it needed to be. She couldn't wait for the second half to begin.

The Flyers came back out onto the field looking recharged and ready to attack. Allie took her usual place at center midfield as the rest of her team lined up.

The Flyers kicked off the second half, carrying the ball down toward the Tornados' goal. But Allie was feeling especially aggressive today. She charged the forward dribbling the ball, in an attempt to steal it. The forward looked up at Allie, surprised, and Allie took her chance to dribble the ball away.

The change in momentum happened so quickly that the Flyers were caught off guard. Allie charged up the open field, her speed working for her as she raced ahead of her opponents, the goal wide open in front of her.

As Allie got closer, she saw the other team's goalie standing with her legs and arms wide apart, prepared to defend the goal. But Allie wasn't deterred. She looked around to see if any of the forwards were open, but she was the only member of her team that far up the field. Thinking quickly, Allie kicked the ball as hard as she could. It flew right over the goalie's head and into the net.

Allie had just scored her first goal as a Tornado!

Allie shrieked in excitement, leaping into the air. She heard the parents in the stands go wild—her own parents louder than all the rest.

"That's my daughter!" she heard her mother exclaim above the applause.

Before she knew it, Jo was tackling her in a bear hug.

"Woooooo!" Jo screamed, a huge dimpled grin on her face.

Marnie ran up, giving her a squeeze. Even Aisha gave Allie a high five. "Nice job!" she said. Allie had never felt a rush like this in all her life.

Allie caught Julie's eye, and Julie gave her a discreet wink from the other end of the field.

As soon as the moment had happened, it was gone, and the game was under way again. Allie refocused, ready to do whatever it took to get her team the win. She even put Julie to the test a few times, tackling her for the ball or zooming past her to pass the ball off to her own forwards.

The Flyers put up an incredible fight, but the Tornados played harder. As the game finished out, the Tornados were ahead 2–1.

Finally, the ref blew the whistle. The families in the stands erupted into cheers. The girls went nuts, gathering together in a huge hug.

"I can't believe it! We're league champions!" Allie exclaimed.

"Thanks in no small part to *you*," Helen said.

"I couldn't have done it without you guys," Allie said.

The Tornados lined up and high-fived the Flyers. They had put up a good fight and looked bummed out to have lost. But they weren't sore losers. They congratulated the Tornados one by one, with smiles on their faces.

Julie grinned at Allie. "Well played," she said. "You were great out there."

"Thanks, Jules," Allie said, unable to hold back her own grin.

Everyone's families came down from the bleachers to celebrate. Allie's parents were giving her congratulatory hugs when she felt a tap on her shoulder.

She turned around to see a boy with shaggy brown hair standing behind her.

"Oh, hey, Thomas," Allie said, blushing. Since she'd gone back to school, she'd seen Thomas in the nurse's office every day at lunch. They didn't talk much, but they said a few shy words from time to time.

Thomas smiled, his big blue eyes lighting up. "I just wanted to say congrats," he said.

Allie smiled. "Thanks," she said.

"I came here to watch my cousin Helen play today," Thomas said. "I didn't know you guys played soccer together. That's cool."

"Yeah," Allie answered. "Helen's the best."

"Well, I guess I'll see you in Nurse Jacobs's office," he said.

"See ya," Allie said, waving.

Thomas turned and walked back to Helen's family. Allie let out a deep breath. Then she caught Helen's eye. She winked at Allie, and then turned back to her parents.

Allie couldn't believe her day. She had scored her first goal, her team won the league championship, *and* a cute boy had told her she did a good job.

"Who was that?" Allie's mom asked. "He was precious."

"Gross, Mom," Allie said, brushing her off. But she couldn't keep a funny, warm feeling from spreading through her stomach.

A few minutes later, the referee approached the Tornados, carrying a huge golden trophy. The statuette on the trophy was of a girl with a long ponytail fiercely kicking a soccer ball.

The plaque on it read: LEAGUE CHAMPIONS.

Chapter 16

"Cheers!" Marnie said, clinking her red plastic cup of soda against her teammates' cups.

"Cheers!" shouted the Tornados.

The girls and their parents were all over at Coach Rebecca's house for their end-of-season banquet. Everyone in the room was in high spirits—particularly Allie. She felt like she was on cloud nine. She couldn't stop smiling!

Coach Rebecca had decorated her sprawling living room in Kelly green. Balloons and streamers were everywhere. Pop music was blasting out of her iPod speakers. Healthy food—and some sweet treats—lined the long table Coach Rebecca had set up.

"Wanna grab some grub?" Jo asked Allie.

"Sure thing," Allie replied, knowing that she had just taken her shot. The two best friends lined up with the other girls, each picking up a green paper plate. Allie loaded hers up with fresh veggies, a ham and cheese wrap, and some fresh fruit. The girls took their plates to a spot on the floor, where the rest of the team sat in smaller groups.

"Hey, Allie," Aisha said, smiling.

"Hey, Aisha," Allie responded. Never in a million years would she have thought it possible, but it seemed like the two of them were becoming friends. Ever since they had talked it out during practice, they'd been chatting on the field, and even at school on occasion. Once you got past her tough exterior, Aisha was actually a really kind and loyal friend.

"You did a nice job playing center mid today," Allie said.

"Thanks," Aisha replied. "You know, I liked it, but I actually think I was better at my old spot. What do you say next season we keep our usual positions, and just switch it up from time to time?"

"Sounds fine to me," Allie smiled. She was nothing if not easygoing. Mostly, she was just happy that she and Aisha were getting along so well.

As Allie sat around talking with her teammates about their season, she began to get a little wistful. The season had come and gone so quickly. She didn't want it to be over.

"So, who's playing indoor soccer this winter?" Marnie asked.

"I am!" several of the girls shouted.

Indoor soccer? Allie thought. Well, maybe she didn't have to worry after all.

Marnie saw the questioning look on Allie's face. "There's an indoor soccer arena downtown," Marnie said. "We can play all winter long!"

"Count me in!" Allie said.

Suddenly, the music quieted down.

"Excuse me!" Coach Rebecca shouted above the noise. "Could I please have your attention for a few minutes?"

A hush fell over the room as the players and their families listened attentively.

"I'd like to take this moment to thank my wonderful team for an amazing season. You girls are the best bunch I've ever had the honor of coaching. Congrats on the win today. You deserved it!"

Helen let out a whoop. Everyone cheered and clapped.

"And now, I'd like to take a moment to hand out a couple of awards," Coach Rebecca said.

Awards? Allie thought. She hadn't heard about this. She noticed that, on the table behind Coach Rebecca, two smaller trophies joined their league championship award.

"First, I'd like to honor this season's most valuable player," Coach Rebecca said. "Without this player, we wouldn't have been able to score nearly as many goals as we did this season. This person is a great team leader, and I'm proud that she's our team captain. Jo Mendes, this award is for you!"

The girls cheered, Allie loudest of all. Jo stood up and walked up to Coach Rebecca, who wrapped her in a hug before handing her the award. No one was surprised that Jo was the MVP. No one played soccer quite like her.

"Now, I'd like to give out a special award to the player who, throughout the course of this season, has made us wonder how we ever got by without her," Coach Rebecca continued. "This girl, while new to our team, has become a true asset, and is an incredible team player. And we all know that, with her diabetes, she had to overcome some obstacles to get to where she got this season. Allie Campbell, you are the Tornados' rookie of the year."

Allie was stunned. After Coach Rebecca hugged her and handed her the award, Allie turned around to face her team and their families. Everyone was on their feet, clapping and cheering for her.

Allie couldn't believe all that had happened to her these past couple of months. Joining a new, elite soccer team. Meeting some of her closest friends. Finding out she had diabetes. She had learned so many valuable lessons, but the most important one was that with a little help from your family and friends, anything was possible.

She could hardly wait for next season.

Questions to Think About

1. When Allie's teammates decide to go out for ice cream, she comes along but doesn't eat any. How does that make her feel? Did you avoid eating anything you liked when you were first diagnosed because you didn't know how to work it in? What do you do now when you want to eat something that you don't know how to work in?

2. Why does Allie decide to keep her diabetes a secret from her friends? Did you wait to tell your friends or did you tell them right away? How did they react when you told them?

3. Allie's first two diabetes education classes are just with her parents, but her third class has two other families in it. Did you have diabetes instruction or classes?

4. Allie says that she feels like her medical ID bracelet is pronouncing her diabetes a bit too loudly. Do you wear some kind of medical ID? How do you feel about wearing it?

5. When Allie returns to school, she says that she may look the same, but she feels like a different person. Did you ever feel that way? Did you talk to anyone about it?

6. Allie is worried that something will go wrong when she goes back to school. Were you nervous about going back to school? What were you most worried about?

7. When Allie goes to the nurse's office for her shot, she finds that another student is waiting for his shot as well. Do you know of anyone else in your school or community who has diabetes?

8. Allie and her parents are learning to plan her meals and snacks. How do you plan what you are going to eat?

9. Allie works out a plan with Coach Rebecca to let her know if she needs to check her blood sugar. Do you play sports? How do you let your coach know if you need a time-out?

10. When Allie first starts playing soccer again, she is distracted by the thought of her diabetes. What sort of obstacles did you encounter when you were first diagnosed? How did you overcome them?

11. Allie is nervous about spending a night away from home so soon after her diagnosis. Have you spent a night away from home yet? Were you nervous? How did you know you were ready?

12. Allie can't wait to have pizza at Charlene's birthday party. What steps does she take to work the pizza into her meal plan? Do you remember your first meal away from home? What steps did you take to plan for it?

13. How did Allie handle her low blood sugar while playing soccer? Do you remember your first low? What happened?

14. Allie and her diabetes nurse work out a schedule for when she should check her blood sugar during the big game. Do you follow a schedule for when you check your blood sugar?

15. Allie is excited to have some cake at the end-of-season banquet. What is your favorite food to treat yourself to? What steps do you take to work it in?

Lilly is an expert in type 1 diabetes, and no one knows families like Disney. Now, these two companies have come together to create special resources for families like yours.

From Lilly Diabetes and Disney Publishing Worldwide comes a series of books for children of different ages and at varying stages of type 1 diabetes. There's also special content for parents of children with type 1 diabetes on Disney's popular website, spoonful.com. Visitors to www.spoonful.com/type1 can find articles, videos, recipes, and tips from caregivers raising children with type 1 diabetes. This unique site highlights ways families can establish new routines and let kids be kids. Together, Lilly's deep expertise in type 1 diabetes and Disney's magic can help keep your child and your family feeling inspired and empowered to live a full, active life with type 1 diabetes! Ask your diabetes healthcare team about getting your hands on the other books in the series and visit www.spoonful.com/type1 today!